S0-CCE-932

LITTLE BITTY MOUSIE

Jim Aylesworth

Illustrations by **Michael Hague**

Walker & Company New York

Sweet Little Bitty Mousie,
Just as cute as cute can be,
Crept into a house one night
To see what she could see.

She saw a shiny **Apple**
In a pretty china bowl.

She climbed to take a nibble,
And she nearly made it roll.

Tip-tip tippy tippy
Went her little mousie toes.
Sniff-sniff sniffy sniffy
Went her little mousie nose.

She licked a stick of **Butter**
That was sitting on a plate.

She bit a bite of **C**arrot,
Which she didn't think was great.

She climbed the dirty **D**ishes
That at dinner held some stew.

She sniffed into an **E**ggshell,
But she found it hard to chew.

Tip-tip tippy tippy
Went her little mousie toes.
Sniff-sniff sniffy sniffy
Went her little mousie nose.

She watched some pretty **F**ishes,
All swimming round and round.

She peeked into the **G**arbage,
Trying not to make a sound.

She ate the "H" from "**H**appy"
On a chocolate birthday cake.

Her fur got full of **Icing**,
And it wasn't by mistake.

Tip-tip tippy tippy
Went her little mousie toes.
Sniff-sniff sniffy sniffy
Went her little mousie nose.

She tried to get some **J**elly—
Tried with all her mousie might.

She also tried the **K**etchup,
But the lids were on too tight.

She found a lady's **Lipstick**
In a shiny golden case.

She looked into a **Mirror**,
But she didn't know her face.

Tip–tip tippy tippy
Went her little mousie toes.
Sniff–sniff sniffy sniffy
Went her little mousie nose.

She sniffed a greasy **N**apkin
That fell from someone's knees.

The peelings of an **O**range
Were mistaken for some cheese.

She took a whiff of **Pepper**,
And it made her double sneeze.

She found a long-lost 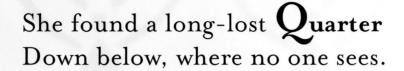Quarter
Down below, where no one sees.

Tip-tip tippy tippy
Went her little mousie toes.
Sniff-sniff sniffy sniffy
Went her little mousie nose.

She climbed to smell some **R**oses,
Being careful of each thorn.

She played inside a **Slipper**
That a little girl had worn.

She found a baby's **Truckie**,
And she tried to take a ride.

She climbed a red **U**mbrella,
And she nearly fell inside.

Tip-tip tippy tippy
Went her little mousie toes.
Sniff-sniff sniffy sniffy
Went her little mousie nose.

She looked up at the **Vacuum**,
And she wondered what it did.

She sniffed a candy **W**rapper
That was thrown down by some kid.

She licked the sugar "**X**'s"
From a dish of hot cross buns.

Some **Yarn**, so soft and fluffy,
Gave her lots and lots of fun.

Tip–tip tippy tippy
Went her little mousie toes.
Sniff–sniff sniffy sniffy
Went her little mousie nose.

She heard the sound of **Z'ing**—
Soft, soft breathing, like a snore.

It came from round the corner,
So she tiptoed cross the floor.

Tip-tip tippy tippy
Went her little mousie toes.
Sniff-sniff sniffy sniffy
Went her little mousie nose.

Sweet Little Bitty Mousie,
Just as scared as scared can be,
Went run run run run running!
That was all she cared to see!

To Rose Fyleman,
who loved mice, and wrote one of my
favorite poems about them.
—J. A.

With love to Jacob Luke, Braden Lee,
Geno Ellias, Mykaela Aneko.
—M. H.

Text copyright © 2007 by Jim Aylesworth
Illustrations copyright © 2007 by Michael Hague

First published in the United States of America in 2007 by Walker Publishing Company, Inc.
Distributed to the trade by Holtzbrinck Publishers

For information about permission to reproduce selections from this book, write to
Permissions, Walker & Company, 104 Fifth Avenue, New York, New York 10011

Library of Congress Cataloging-in-Publication Data
Aylesworth, Jim.
Little Bitty Mousie / Jim Aylesworth ; illustrated by Michael Hague.
p.   cm.
Summary: Little Bitty Mousie sneaks into a house one night and
discovers many tantalizing new things, as well as one very scary thing.
ISBN-13: 978-0-8027-9637-0 • ISBN-10: 0-8027-9637-0 (hardcover)
ISBN-13: 978-0-8027-9638-7 • ISBN-10: 0-8027-9638-9 (reinforced)
[1. Mice—Fiction. 2. Stories in rhyme.] I. Hague, Michael, ill. II. Title.
PZ8.3.A95Lit 2007   [E]—dc22   2007002366

Book design by Donna Mark
Typeset in Mrs Eaves
The pictures for this book were drawn in pencil
then scanned and colored in Photoshop.

Visit Walker & Company's Web site at www.walkeryoungreaders.com

Printed in China
2 4 6 8 10 9 7 5 3 1 (hardcover)
2 4 6 8 10 9 7 5 3 1 (reinforced)

All papers used by Walker & Company are natural, recyclable products
made from wood grown in well-managed forests. The manufacturing processes
conform to the environmental regulations of the country of origin.